THUNDERBIRDS™

ARE GO

DARE AND RESCUE STICKER BOOK

The challenge starts here...

In case of emergency, check your answers on page 47.

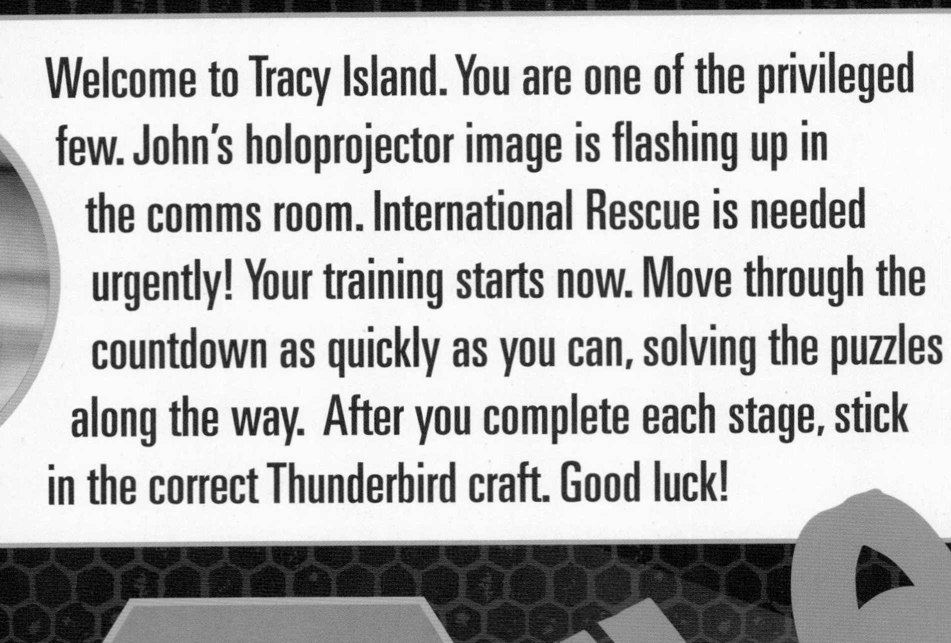

Welcome to Tracy Island. You are one of the privileged few. John's holoprojector image is flashing up in the comms room. International Rescue is needed urgently! Your training starts now. Move through the countdown as quickly as you can, solving the puzzles along the way. After you complete each stage, stick in the correct Thunderbird craft. Good luck!

5

Follow the arrows, then name the world security force operating in 2060.

L D L F O C E E B R E N G F E O A C

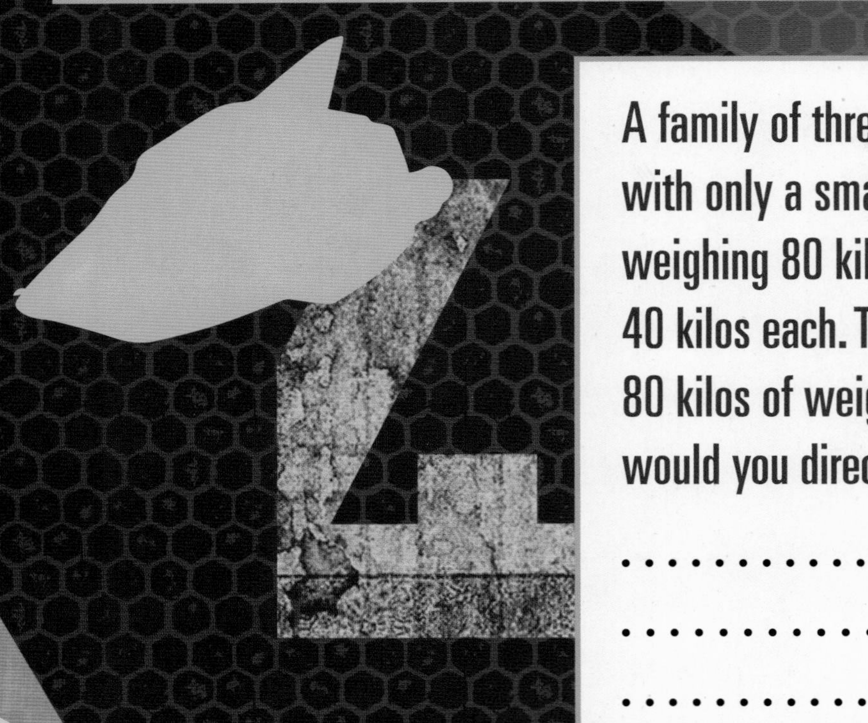

4

A family of three are stranded on an island, with only a small raft. There is a man weighing 80 kilos and two youths, weighing 40 kilos each. The raft can only bear 80 kilos of weight at one time. How would you direct the family to safety?

. . . .

. . . .

. . . .

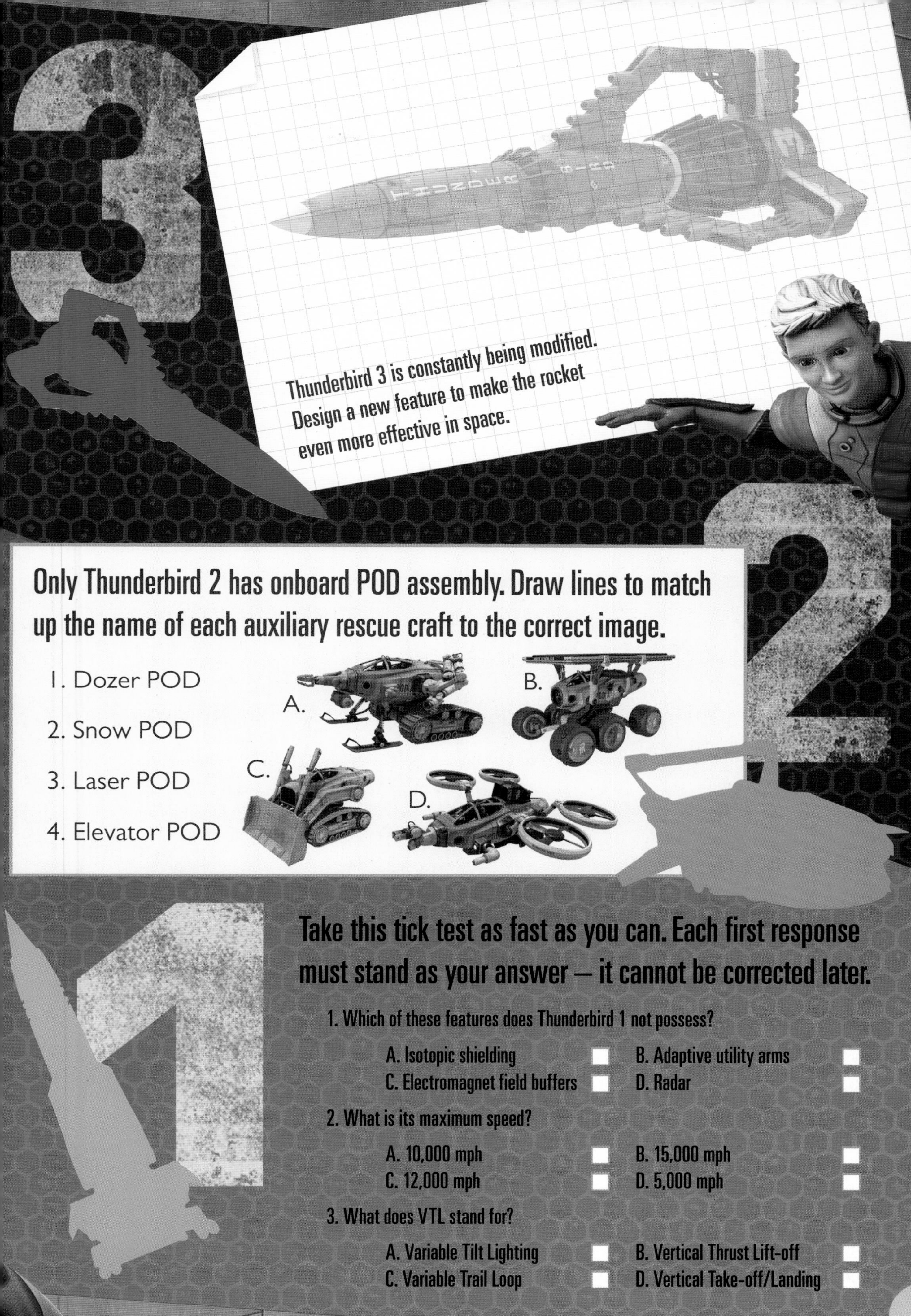

Thunderbird 3 is constantly being modified. Design a new feature to make the rocket even more effective in space.

Only Thunderbird 2 has onboard POD assembly. Draw lines to match up the name of each auxiliary rescue craft to the correct image.

1. Dozer POD
2. Snow POD
3. Laser POD
4. Elevator POD

A.

B.

C.

D.

Take this tick test as fast as you can. Each first response must stand as your answer – it cannot be corrected later.

1. Which of these features does Thunderbird 1 not possess?

   A. Isotopic shielding ☐ B. Adaptive utility arms ☐
   C. Electromagnet field buffers ☐ D. Radar ☐

2. What is its maximum speed?

   A. 10,000 mph ☐ B. 15,000 mph ☐
   C. 12,000 mph ☐ D. 5,000 mph ☐

3. What does VTL stand for?

   A. Variable Tilt Lighting ☐ B. Vertical Thrust Lift-off ☐
   C. Variable Trail Loop ☐ D. Vertical Take-off/Landing ☐

THUNDERBIRDS ARE GO

Three of the team are scrambling to their vehicles, ready to rescue where all else has failed. Which Tracy brothers are answering the call of duty this time? Study each of the clue chains, then stick the right photo I.D. at the bottom.

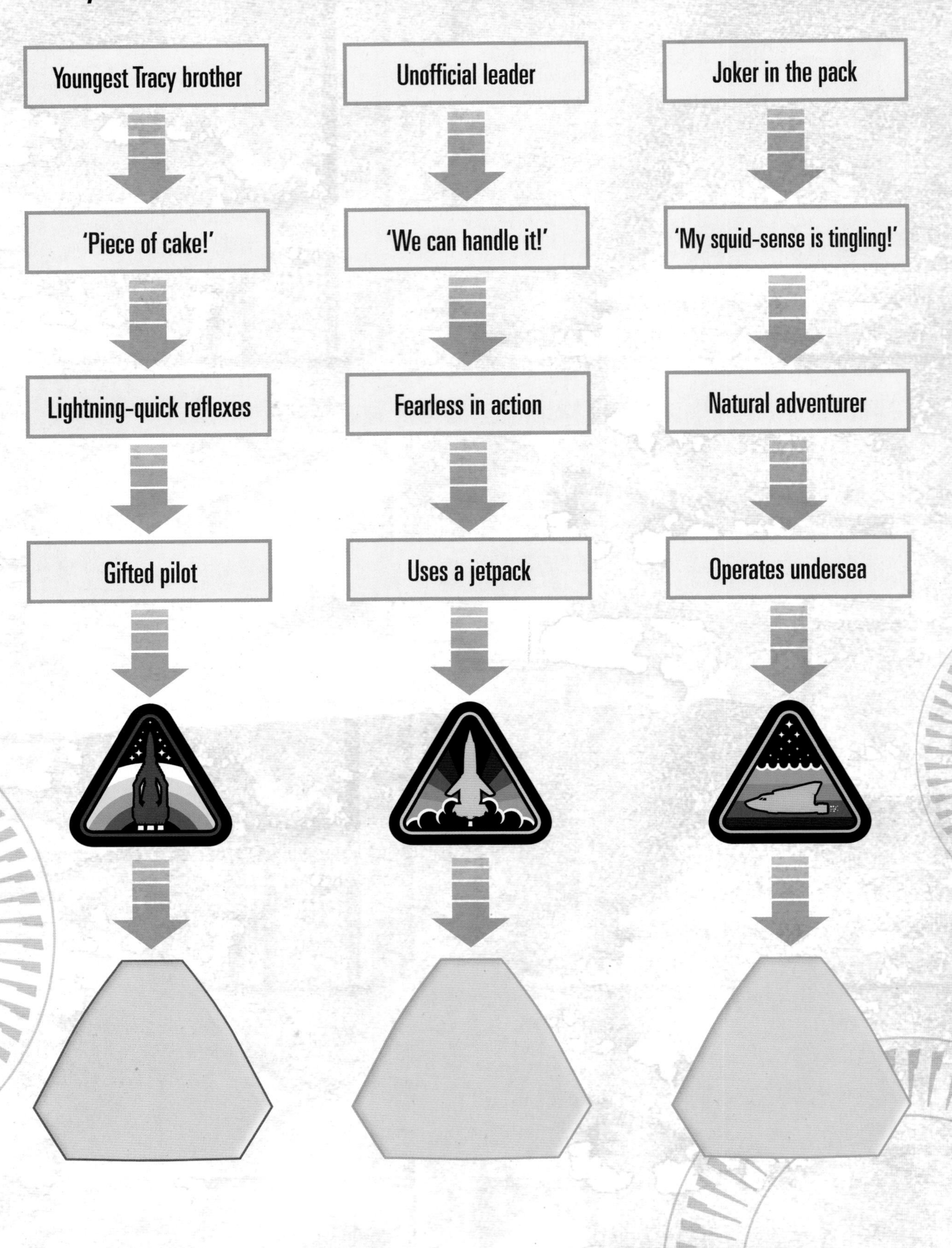

SECURITY BREACH

Kayo runs the security for International Rescue. Over the years, she has learned never to take any chances. When a dubious surveillance device appears in the grounds of Tracy Island, Kayo destroys it immediately.

Whose face is flickering across the shattered screen? Circle the missing shards, then use your stickers to piece the picture back together again.

Kayo trains all of the Tracy brothers in self-defence. She is a master of Wing Chun martial arts.

TUNNELS OF TIME

Lady Penelope, Parker and Gordon are trapped inside an ancient Amazonian Temple. The place is dark, dusty and heavily booby-trapped. Can you help Virgil guide the trio to a safe rescue location? Follow his instructions to the letter!

Put your finger on the green radar pulse showing the captives' current location. Now move five metres east, three metres north, nine metres west and one metre south. The rescue location is marked with a letter. Write it here ___

1 grid square = 1 metre

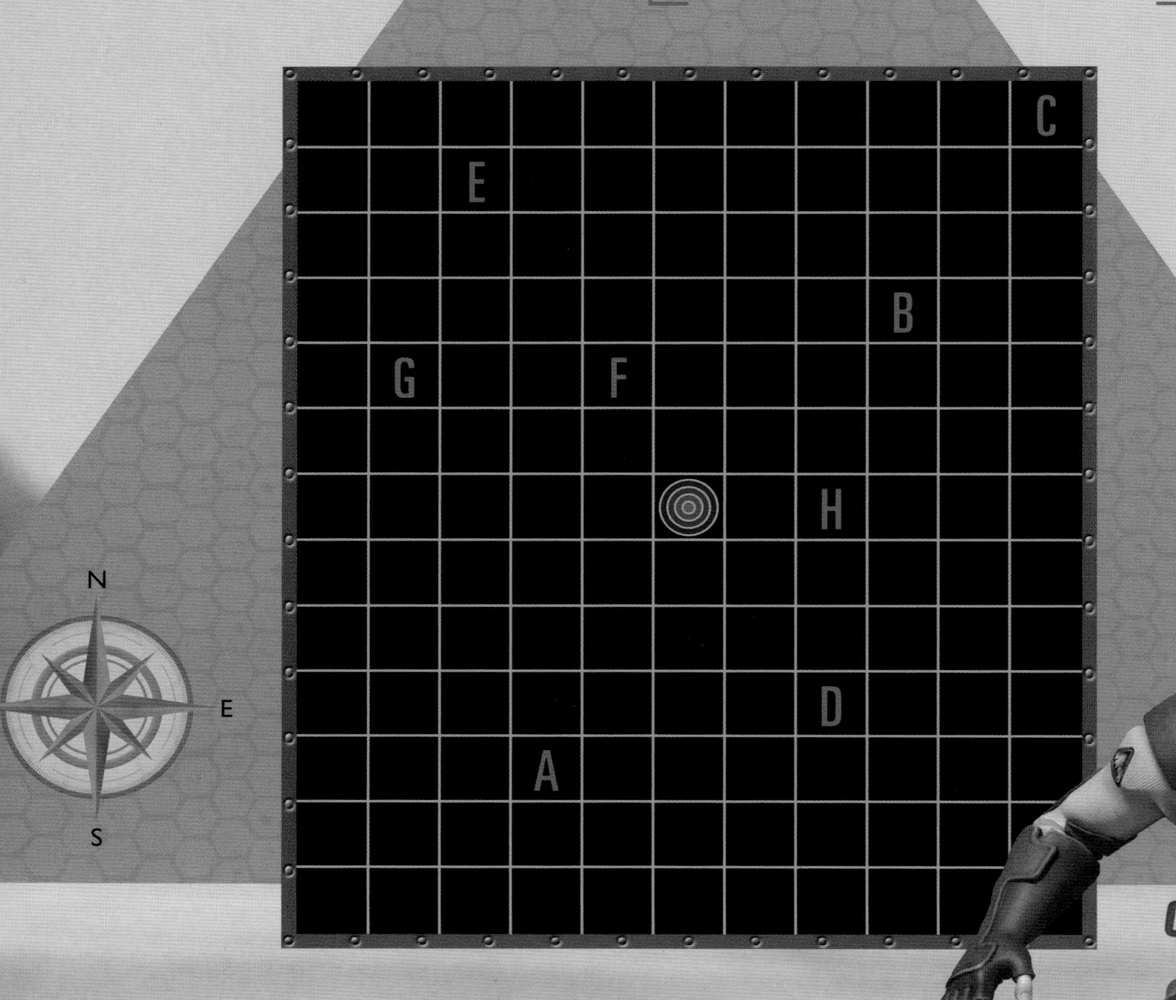

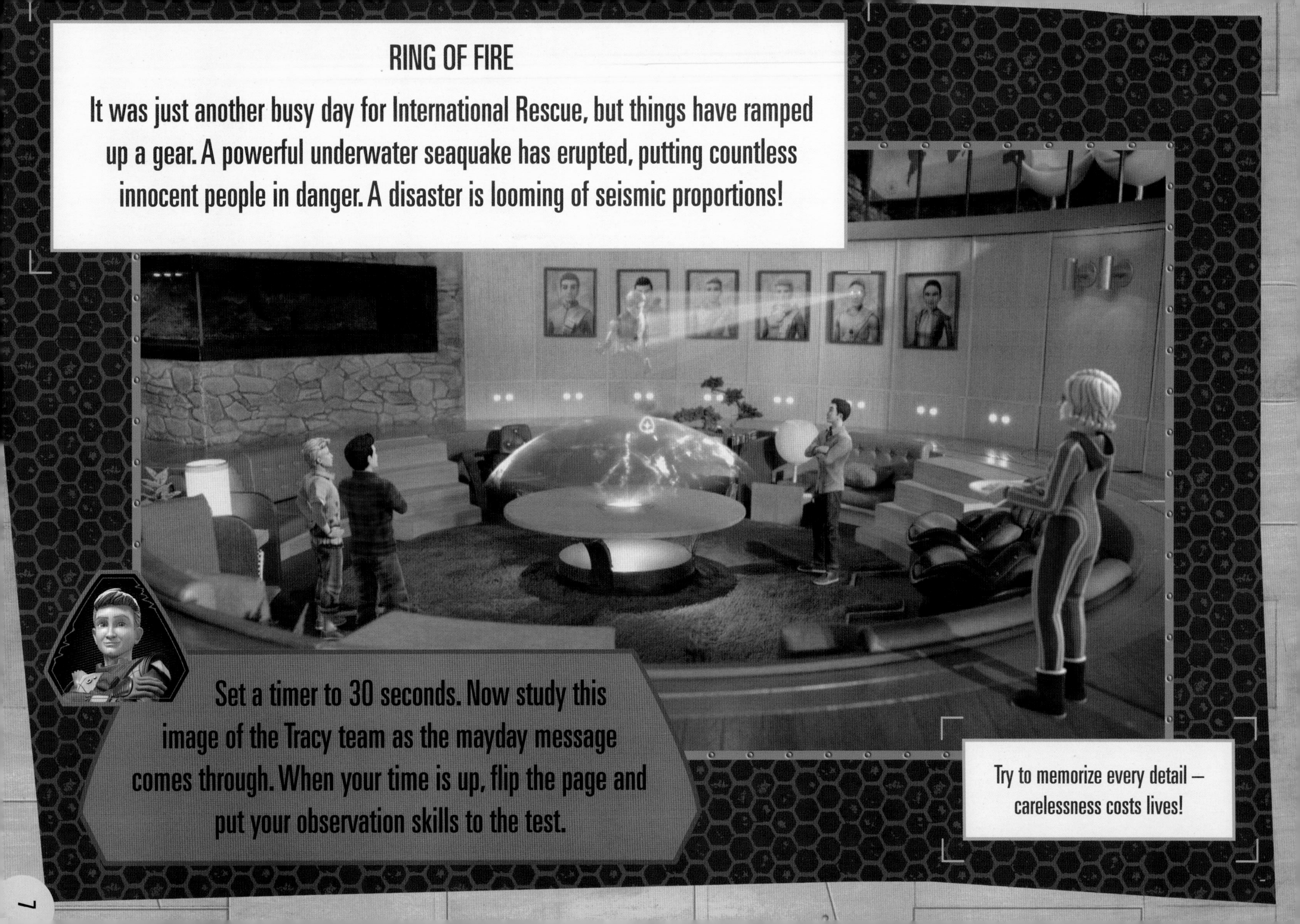

RING OF FIRE

It was just another busy day for International Rescue, but things have ramped up a gear. A powerful underwater seaquake has erupted, putting countless innocent people in danger. A disaster is looming of seismic proportions!

Set a timer to 30 seconds. Now study this image of the Tracy team as the mayday message comes through. When your time is up, flip the page and put your observation skills to the test.

Try to memorize every detail – carelessness costs lives!

Work your way through the quiz questions below.
THUNDERBIRDS ARE GO

1. How many Tracy brothers have gathered in the comms room?

....

2. What colour is the carpet in the centre?

....

3. What is Grandma Tracy holding?

....

4. Which brother is projecting onto the holo-screen?

....

5. Who is standing next to Virgil?

....

6. How many framed pictures are lining the back wall?

....

7. What colour is Gordon's shirt?

....

8. What is Grandma Tracy wearing on her feet?

....

When you've finished, check your answers on page 47. If you scored more than six, stick the International Rescue sign here.

International Rescue has friends in high places – a handful of brave and unsung individuals that work tirelessly behind the scenes. The Creighton-Ward estate in England is a hub of covert activity. Stick in photos and unscramble words to reveal who or what you might see behind its impressive gates.

SPACE SPECS

Two International Rescue vehicles push the reaches of science to its very limits! Thunderbird 3 and Thunderbird 5 are high-tech, low-emission spacecrafts, each designed to fulfill a unique role for the organization.

What features do each of the vehicles have? Read each spec feature, then draw a line to match it to the correct Thunderbird.

THUNDERBIRD 3
FUNCTION: SPACE RESCUE AND LOGISTICS HUB

1. ROTATING GRAVITY RING

2. SPACE ELEVATOR

3. FINE POSITIONING NOZZLES

4. OBSERVATION DECK

5. PRIMARY AND SECONDARY THRUSTERS

6. HANGAR BAY

7. DRILL EQUIPMENT

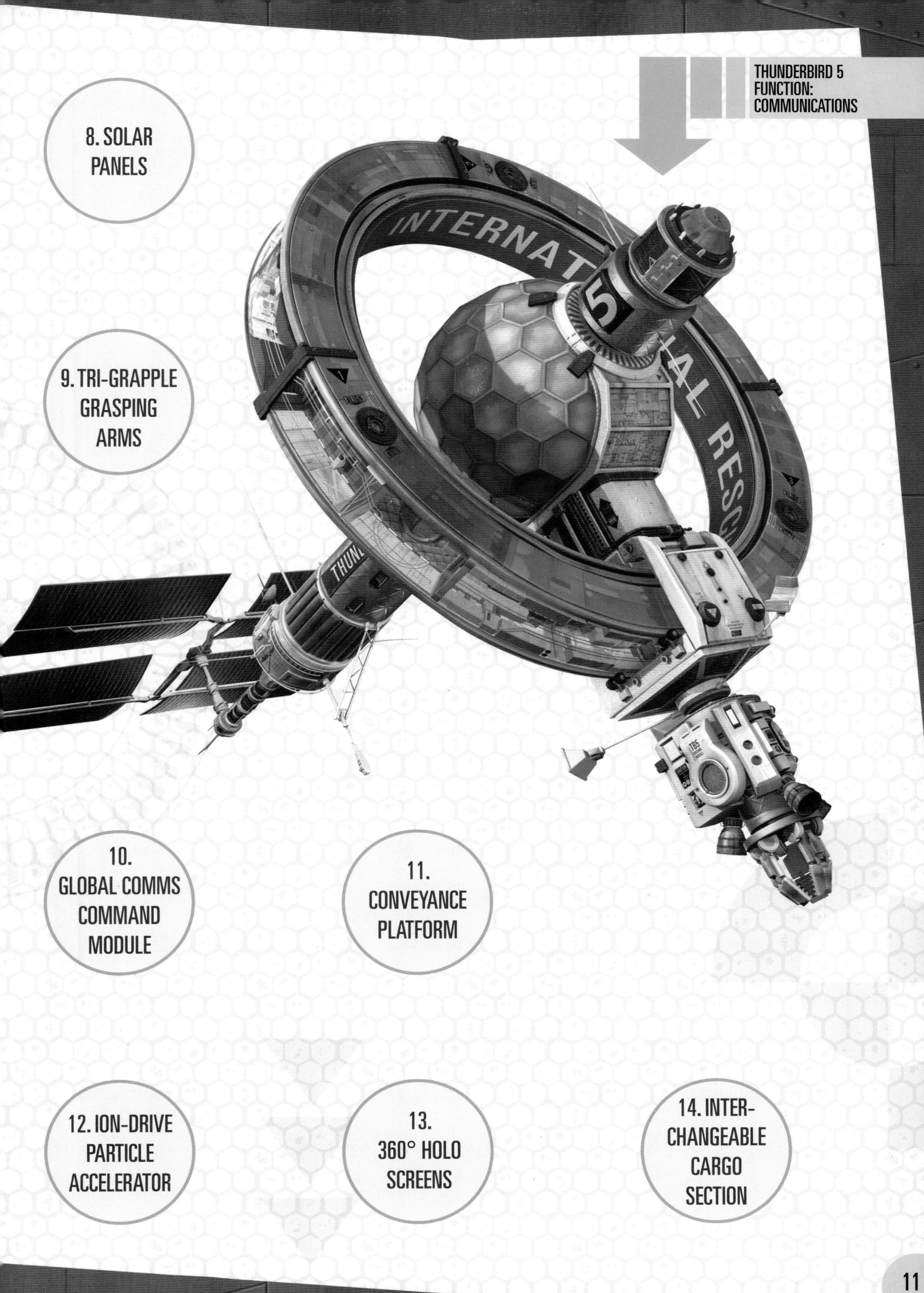
THUNDERBIRD 5
FUNCTION:
COMMUNICATIONS
8. SOLAR PANELS
9. TRI-GRAPPLE GRASPING ARMS
10. GLOBAL COMMS COMMAND MODULE
11. CONVEYANCE PLATFORM
12. ION-DRIVE PARTICLE ACCELERATOR
13. 360° HOLO SCREENS
14. INTER-CHANGEABLE CARGO SECTION
INTERNAT AL RESC
5

GADGET GRID

Brains is a science genius, working night and day to provide the Tracy brothers with cutting edge technology. He's happiest in his lab, quietly tinkering with machines and vehicle parts. Take a look at Brains' latest invention – a puzzle for new recruits! Think coolly and carefully, then use your stickers to crack it.

TASK: Fill the entire gadget grid with stickers.
PROTOCOL: Each mini-box should contain six unique gadgets. No gadget may feature more than once in each row, column or mini-box.

Nothing is impossible if you use your Brain!

DOUBLE CROSSER

Scott needs urgent assistance – someone has hacked into Thunderbird 1's on-board computer! All incoming messages have become encrypted. Can you step in and decipher Scott's next order?

W	M	M	G	K	U	D	E	U	P
J	U	R	S	X	I	Z	X	O	Q
B	J	Y	B	N	B	S	S	N	J
N	S	C	V	M	B	Z	T	B	M
K	A	X	H	Q	J	C	N	C	D
G	V	D	N	F	Y	V	G	K	L

Work your way across the screen, crossing out any letters that appear more than twice. Write the remaining ones here ....

Now combine your logic and initiative to unscramble the letters.

What is the message for Thunderbird 1? W _ _ _ F _ _ H _ _ _

TRACY ISLAND FLY BY

To innocent eyes, Tracy Island looks like a very expensive, and very private, holiday resort. Its real function is much more intriguing. Use your stickers to fill the skies above the hideaway with International Rescue vehicles.

COVERT OPS

Quiet and ever watchful, Kayo is a force to be reckoned with. How much do you know about International Rescue's most secret weapon? Pit your wits against this top secret tick test. How high can you score?

1. Kayo was born in...
   - A. England ☐
   - B. Tahiti ☐
   - C. USA ☐
   - D. Tracy Island ☐

2. Her full name is...
   - A. Tanusha Kranos ☐
   - B. Tanusha Kindle ☐
   - C. Tanusha Kronos ☐
   - D. Tanusha Kyrano ☐

3. Kayo is an expert in...
   - A. Bobsledding ☐
   - B. Fencing ☐
   - C. Kung Fu ☐
   - D. Mud Wrestling ☐

4. Kayo is tasked with managing Tracy Island's...
   - A. Catering ☐
   - B. Transport ☐
   - C. Security ☐
   - D. IT Connections ☐

5. Kayo took over the job from her...
   - A. Father ☐
   - B. Mother ☐
   - C. Sister ☐
   - D. Cousin ☐

6. Kayo's mission suit features an integral...
   - A. Pressure Regulator ☐
   - B. Stun Gun ☐
   - C. Jetpack ☐
   - D. Parasail ☐

7. Kayo pilots a...
   - A. Supersonic Jet ☐
   - B. Helicopter ☐
   - C. Stealth Jet ☐
   - D. Holofoil ☐

8. Thunderbird S is also known as...
   - A. The Hawk ☐
   - B. The Shadow ☐
   - C. The Cloud ☐
   - D. The Ghost ☐

AERIAL ASSISTANCE

The Hood and his operatives have broken into a secret US state facility in the middle of the desert. Thunderbird 2 has been scrambled to the location. Can you help Virgil find the quickest flight path? This will be the route through the least number of squares.

Directive: It is only safe to travel across the green grid squares.

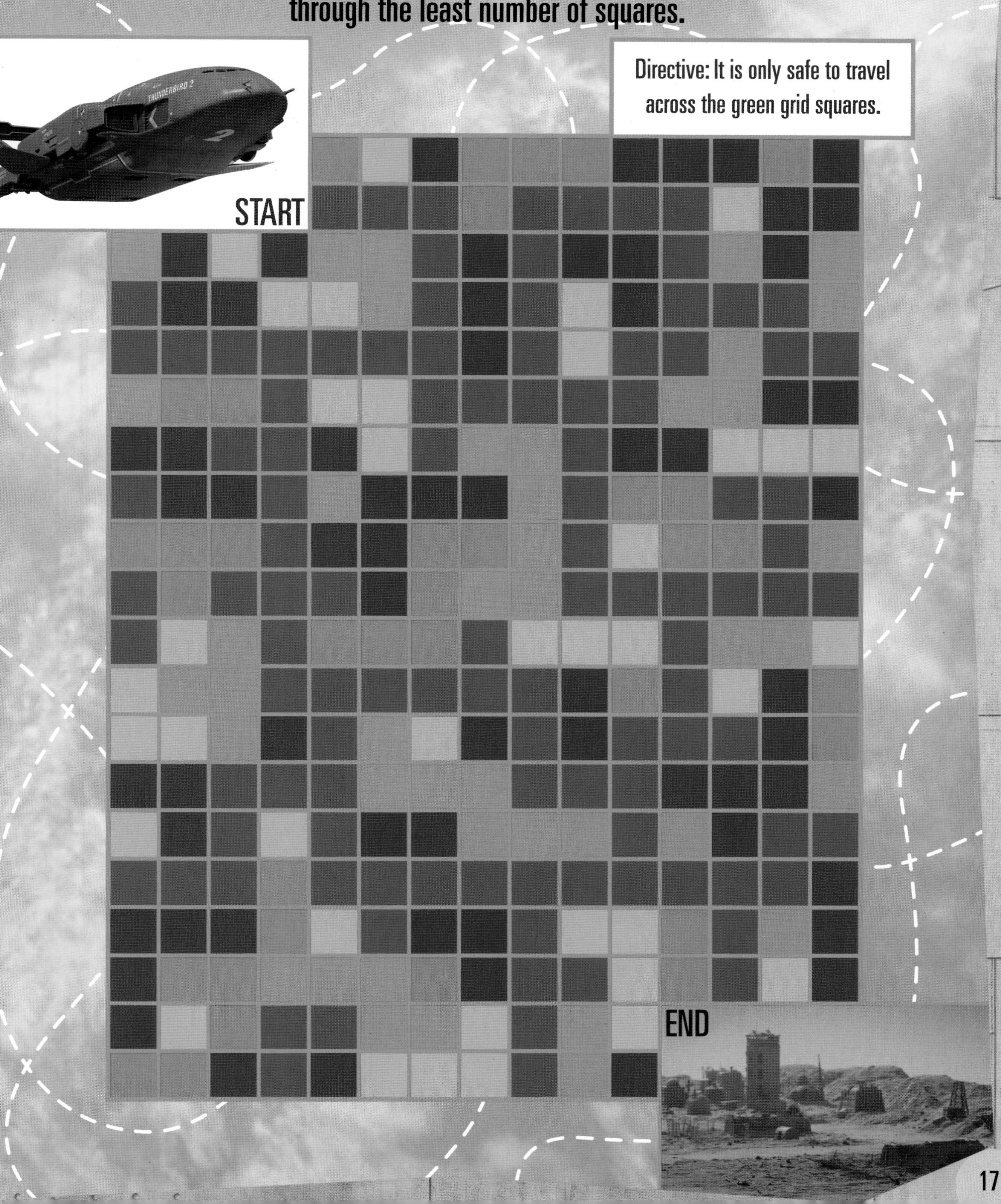

PRIVATE AND CONFIDENTIAL

When the Global Defence Force runs out of ideas, International Rescue steps in! The team of Kayo, Brains, Lady Penelope, Parker and of course the five Tracy brothers, is there to save the day. But there is one other important figure in IR, who is missing in action and whose identity remains classified. Can you crack the code, reveal the secret ID and find out their role in shaping International Rescue? Write the correct name beside each picture, then add the boxed letters to the message grid.

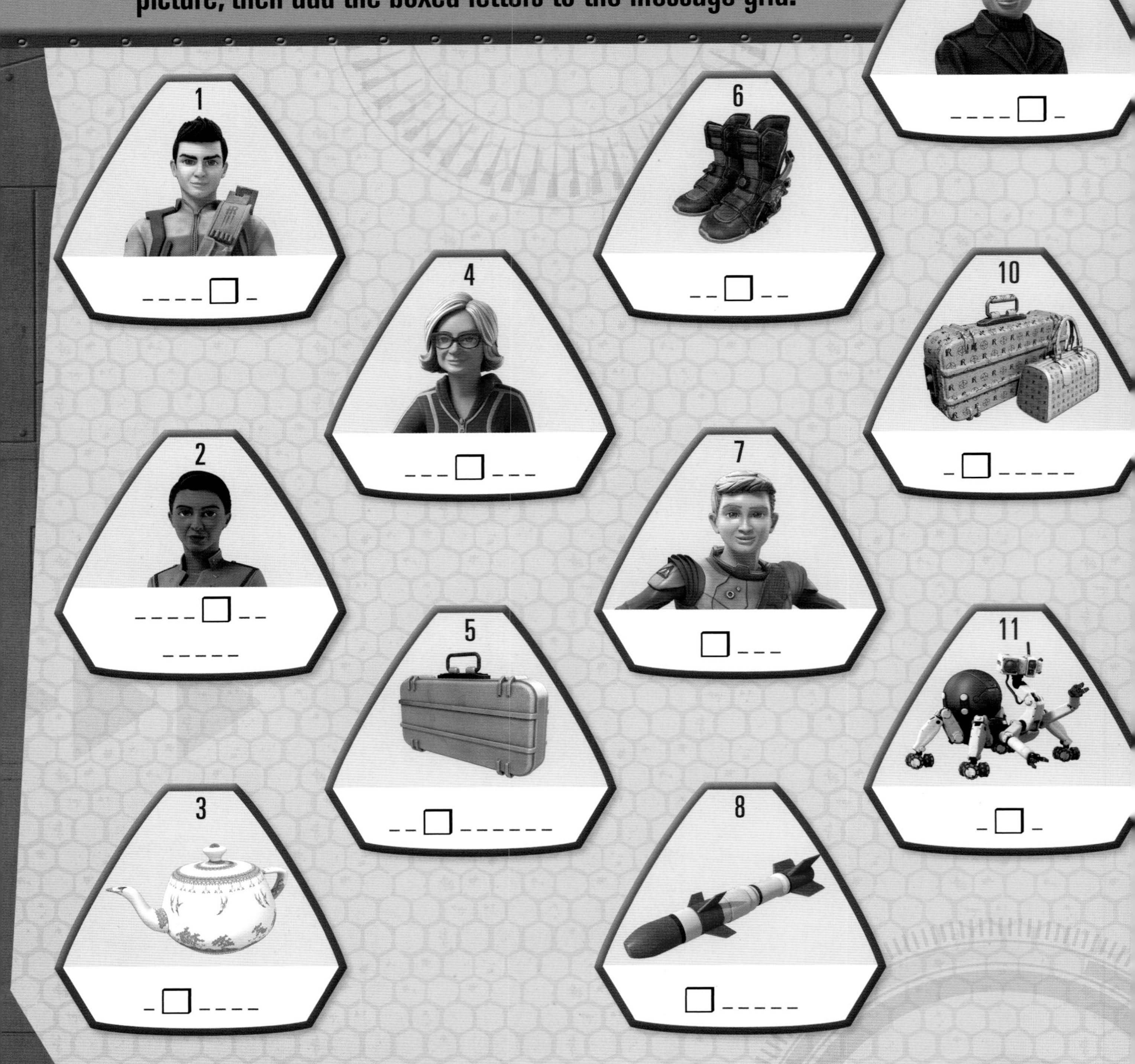

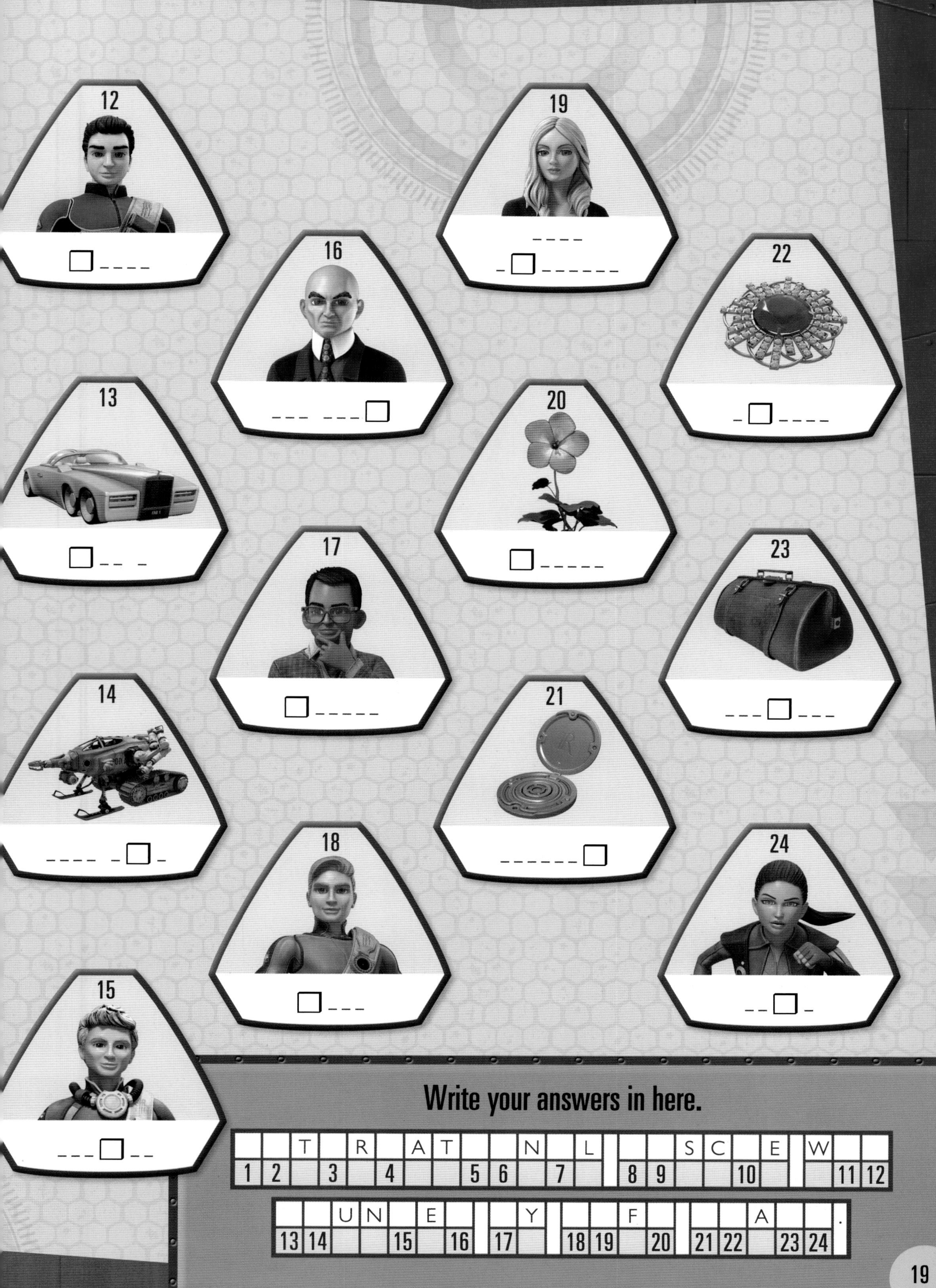
12
19
16
22
13
20
17
23
14
21
18
24
15
Write your answers in here.
T R A T N L S C E W
1 2 3 4 5 6 7 8 9 10 11 12
U N E Y F A .
13 14 15 16 17 18 19 20 21 22 23 24

Sometimes the Thunderbirds are tested to their absolute limits. Read about this daring space rescue, then stick in the missing pictures.

1. The residents of Tracy Island were celebrating an unusual Thanksgiving – International Rescue had lasted 48 hours without a major global emergency! John decided to take the space elevator back up to Thunderbird 5.

5. CIR.R.U.S was reaching dangerously high altitudes. Scott flew Thunderbird 1 as close to the station as he dared. He used a grapple pulley to connect with the station, but the zipline snapped. Rescue aborted!

4. Gordon and Virgil prepared Thunderbird 2 for take-off. Within minutes the transporter was approaching the CIR.R.U.S weather station. Gordon tried to close in using the repair POD, but the air was too turbulent!

9. Slowly and surely, Thunderbird 5 began t winch CIR.R.U.S. up into space. The gravity ring around the craft spun faster and faste The intense G-force knocked John off hi feet. He collapsed on the flight deck flo

8. John pushed his rocket thrusters up to the max, determined to get close to CIR.R.U.S. After pulling off a complex manoeuvre, Thunderbird 5 managed to extend its space elevator down towards the weather station.

. But over in the Indian Ocean, a hurricane was ewing. CIR.R.U.S, a high tech climate research crew, lt the effects in their weather station. The CIR.R.U.S ation suddenly began to rise in altitude.

3. Storm winds had shorted out the heli-blades that helped the weather station maintain a safe cruising height. IR had a situation on its hands after all! John used the holoprojector to alert the other Tracy brothers.

6. Alan launched Thunderbird 3. The rocket positioned itself precariously underneath CIR.R.U.S. Alan tried to clamp onto the station and pull it downwards, but a piece of the framework broke away.

7. Alan and the other Thunderbirds had to pull away from the weather station. International Rescue was running out of options. Brains had one last-ditch plan – for John to mount a remote space rescue from Thunderbird 5!

10. Just when the situation was looking bleak, CIR.R.U.S. was pulled into orbit. John used all his strength to hit the controls and move Thunderbird 5 to safety. It was the end of a long night – mission accomplished!

SYSTEM CRASH

EOS, the artificial intelligence programme that co-controls Thunderbird 5, is malfunctioning! Examine the pixelated comms screens. Can you make out who is trying to make contact? Write the correct name underneath each screen.

....

....

....

....

....

....

M.A.X. MADNESS

Have you met M.A.X.? Brains' robotic assistant is constantly by his side, ready to fix appliances, service vehicles or test out a new prototype. Brains wants you create a portrait of M.A.X., but as usual the engineer has decided to make things a little more challenging.

The colour copy grid at the top of the page has been encrypted. Find a pencil and then copy the contents of each number square into the matching number square in the empty grid below. Have you got a cool head and the art skills to get M.A.X. activation ready?

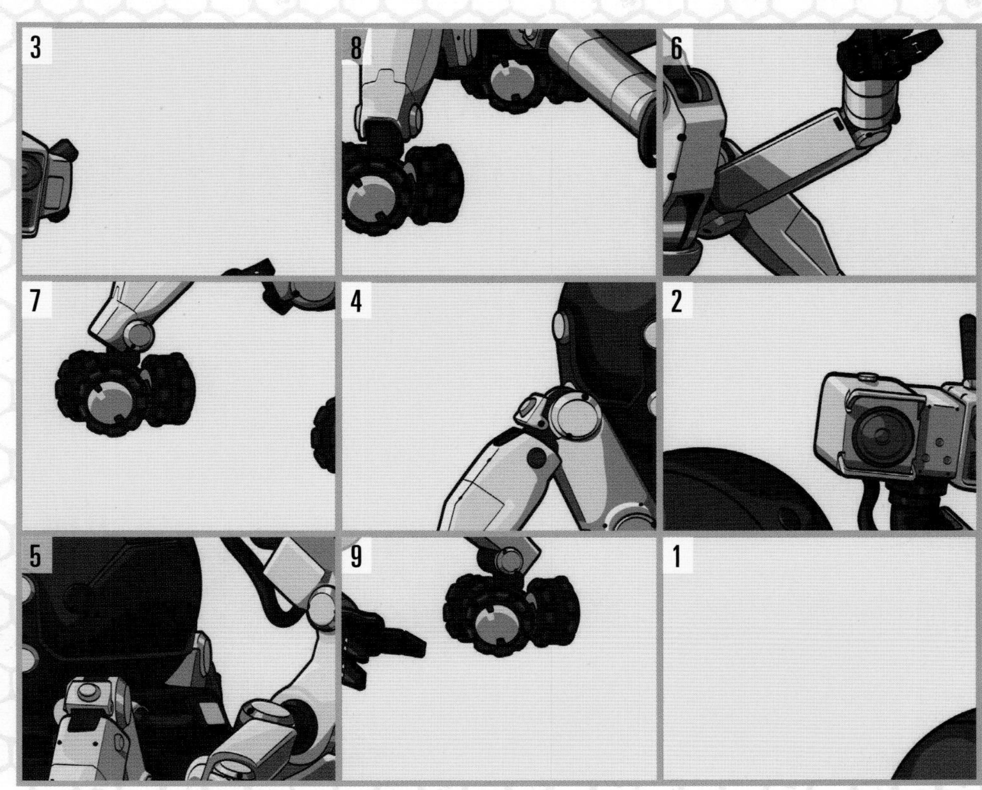

International Rescue operatives are high-functioning, focussed and used to handling pressure. How about you? Can you solve this nerve-fraying crossword puzzle without losing your cool? You have ten minutes. Read the clues, then write the answers into the crossword grid.

ACROSS

1. Jeff Tracy is _ _ _ _ _ _ _.
2. Strong pilot of Thunderbird 2.
3. What the Tracy team does every day.
4. The adapted mirrored device that Lady Penelope uses as a high tech video link.
5. The extinct natural phenomenon that Tracy Island is built on.
6. Lady Penelope's beloved pet dog.
7. Ex-bodyguard Parker's other former job.
8. Head of security for International Rescue.
9. Thunderbird 4's domain.
10. The colour of FAB 1.

DOWN

1. Grandma Tracy's least successful hobby.
2. Chief commanding officer for the Global Defence Force.
3. Brains' function at International Rescue.
4. The number of Tracy brothers.
5. The environment that John usually operates in.
6. The eldest Tracy brother.
7. Sleepy Alan likes to take a lot of these.
8. The reach of the International Rescue team.
9. Lady Penelope's nationality.
10. A computer programme used on Thunderbird 5.

THUNDERBIRD 4
4
2
THUNDERBIRD 2
TB
THUNDERBIRD
1
TB
3
THUNDERBIRD
1
2
3
4
5
7
8
7
9
10
FAB 1

THUNDERBIRD
TB 1 TB
THUNDERBIRD 2

PARKER
VIRGIL TRACY
LADY PENELOPE
BRAINS
THE HOOD
GRANDMA
KAYO
JOHN TRACY
THUNDERBIRD 4
TB1
THUNDERBIRD 2
THUNDERBIRD
SCOTT TRACY
GORDON TRACY
VIRGIL TRACY
JOHN TRACY
ALAN TRACY

LADY PENELOPE
VIRGIL
PARKER
ALAN
BRAINS
GORDON
JOHN
KAYO
SCOTT
T2

1
2
7
3
10
8
8
6
9
9
THUNDERBIRD
4

SECRET SURVEILLANCE

It's time to test your acting skills! Read the eight lines of communication below out loud. Think as you read – do the words remind you of anyone? There are eight name badges on the sticker sheets in the middle of the book. Peel off each one, then stick it beside the correct name.

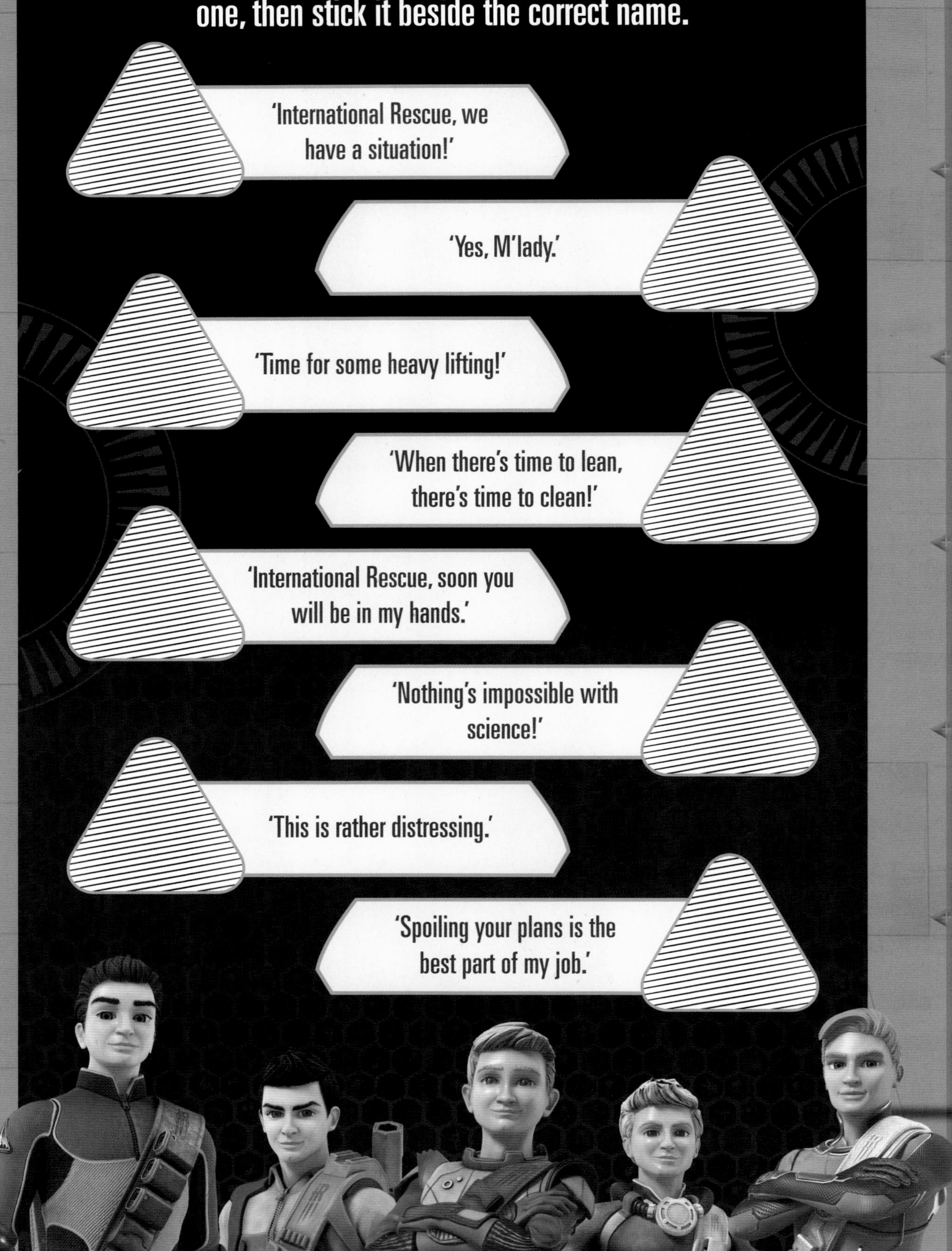

SPACE RACE

Lady Penelope and Parker are on a desperate mission – to sneak into a top secret storage facility and find the mine's deactivation code! The code is made up of six symbols, hiding somewhere in a network of data. Locate and circle it.

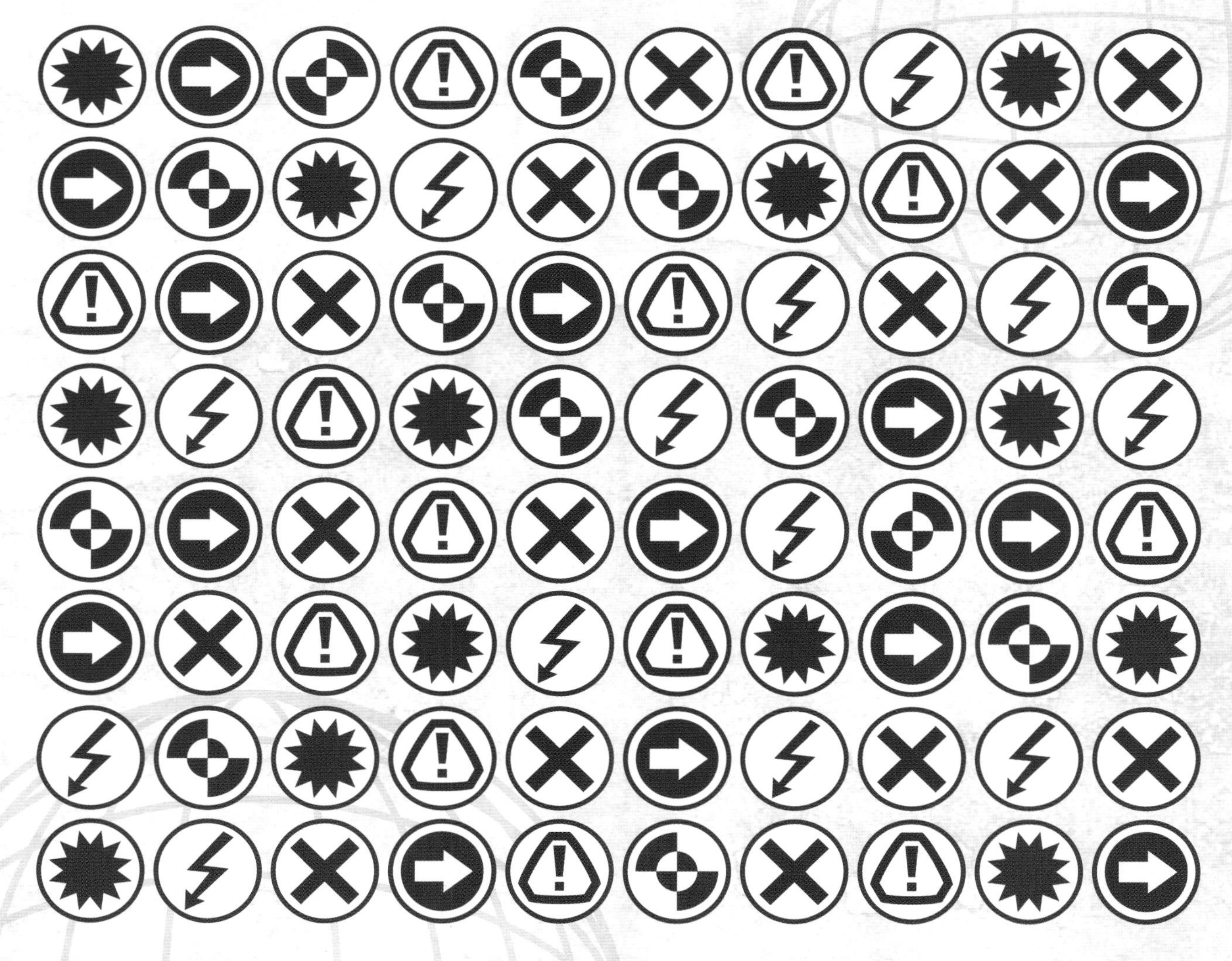

SCRAMBLE!

John Tracy has a crucial role – as well as piloting the Thunderbird 5 orbital space station, he serves as Mission Control for International Rescue. Can you give him some much needed back-up? Assess each of these rescues, then stick in the correct vehicle required.

1
The ocean floor has been destabilised by a series of seaquakes. A research centre located in a deep ocean trench has become unsafe for the scientists on board.

2
There's been an explosion deep underground in an industrial diamond mine. International Rescue will need to bore through rock to reach the survivors.

3
Air traffic control above the Americas has been disrupted, plunging flights into chaos. A secret surveillance mission is needed to find out the source of the disturbance.

4
An unusual radiation spike has been
picked up from a remote corner of Africa,
consistent with a uranium leak.
The potential consequences are dire –
International Rescue has to get there fast!
5
The GDF has deployed
a fake convoy to distract
The Hood, supposedly carrying a
prototype generator. While he's kept
busy, the real prototype needs a motor
escort to deliver it safely.
6
A meteor shower is
projected to hit the Shadow Alpha
One Moon Base. International Rescue need to
land a vehicle onto the surface of the Moon
and rescue the base's crew member.

BRAIN BURN

Thunderbird 1 is getting ready for blast-off! The rocket is powerful enough to reach any location on Earth in less than 30 minutes. Help Alan prepare by scaling this word grid. Start at the top, changing one letter on each line to morph one word into a new one.

ALAN

A method for achiving an end. _ _ _ _

Put on in a theatre. _ _ _ _

A clever trick. _ _ _ _

To plan secretly. _ _ _ _

A narrow opening. _ _ _ _

Narrow strips of wood. _ _ _ _

Something that you sit on. _ _ _ _

HEAT

STICKER THIS!

OK recruit, ready for a quick reaction sticker quiz?
Top-notch operatives will be able to fill in this page in less than five minutes.
Read the definitions, search for the correct pictures and get sticking!

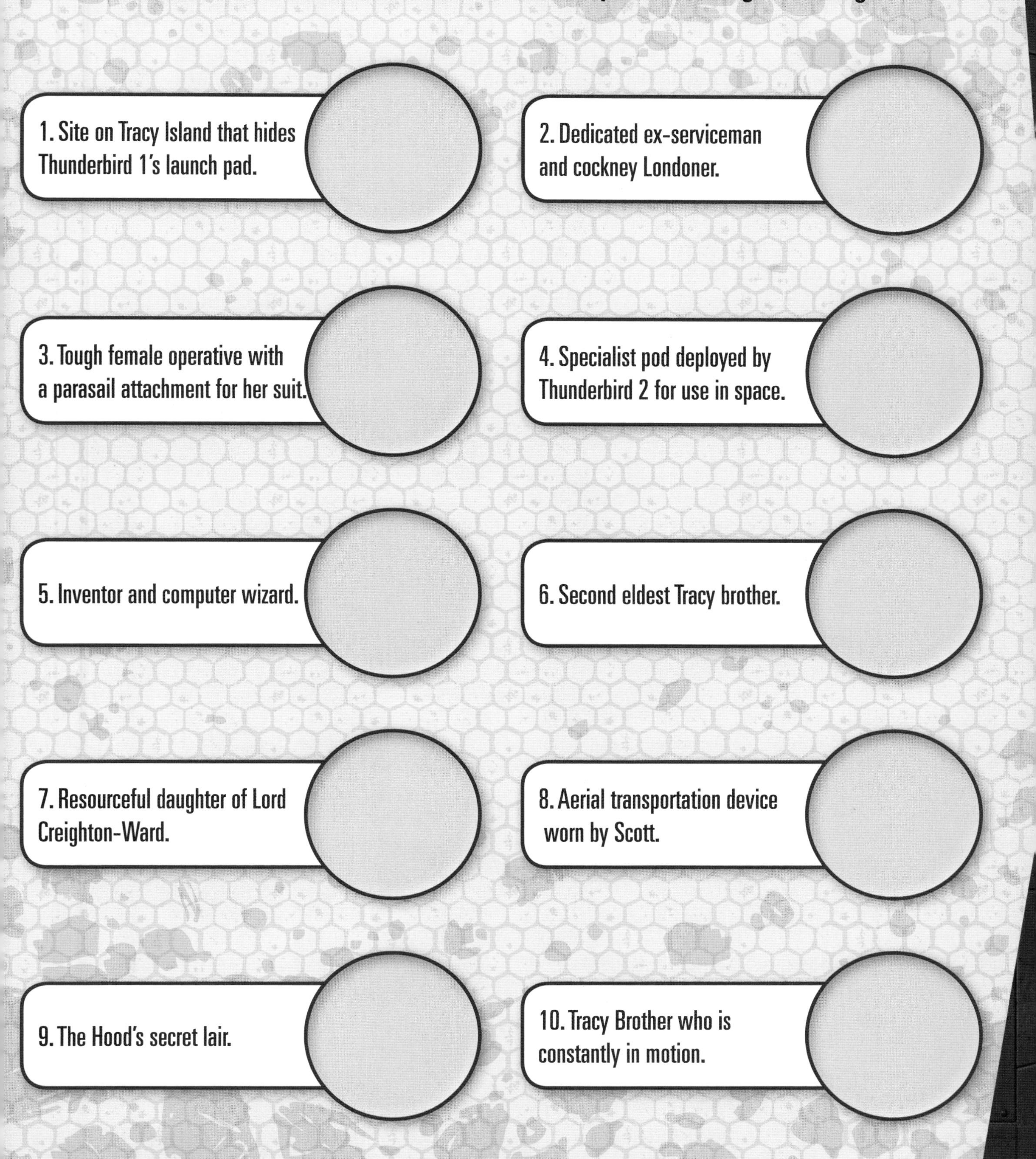

1. Site on Tracy Island that hides Thunderbird 1's launch pad.

2. Dedicated ex-serviceman and cockney Londoner.

3. Tough female operative with a parasail attachment for her suit.

4. Specialist pod deployed by Thunderbird 2 for use in space.

5. Inventor and computer wizard.

6. Second eldest Tracy brother.

7. Resourceful daughter of Lord Creighton-Ward.

8. Aerial transportation device worn by Scott.

9. The Hood's secret lair.

10. Tracy Brother who is constantly in motion.

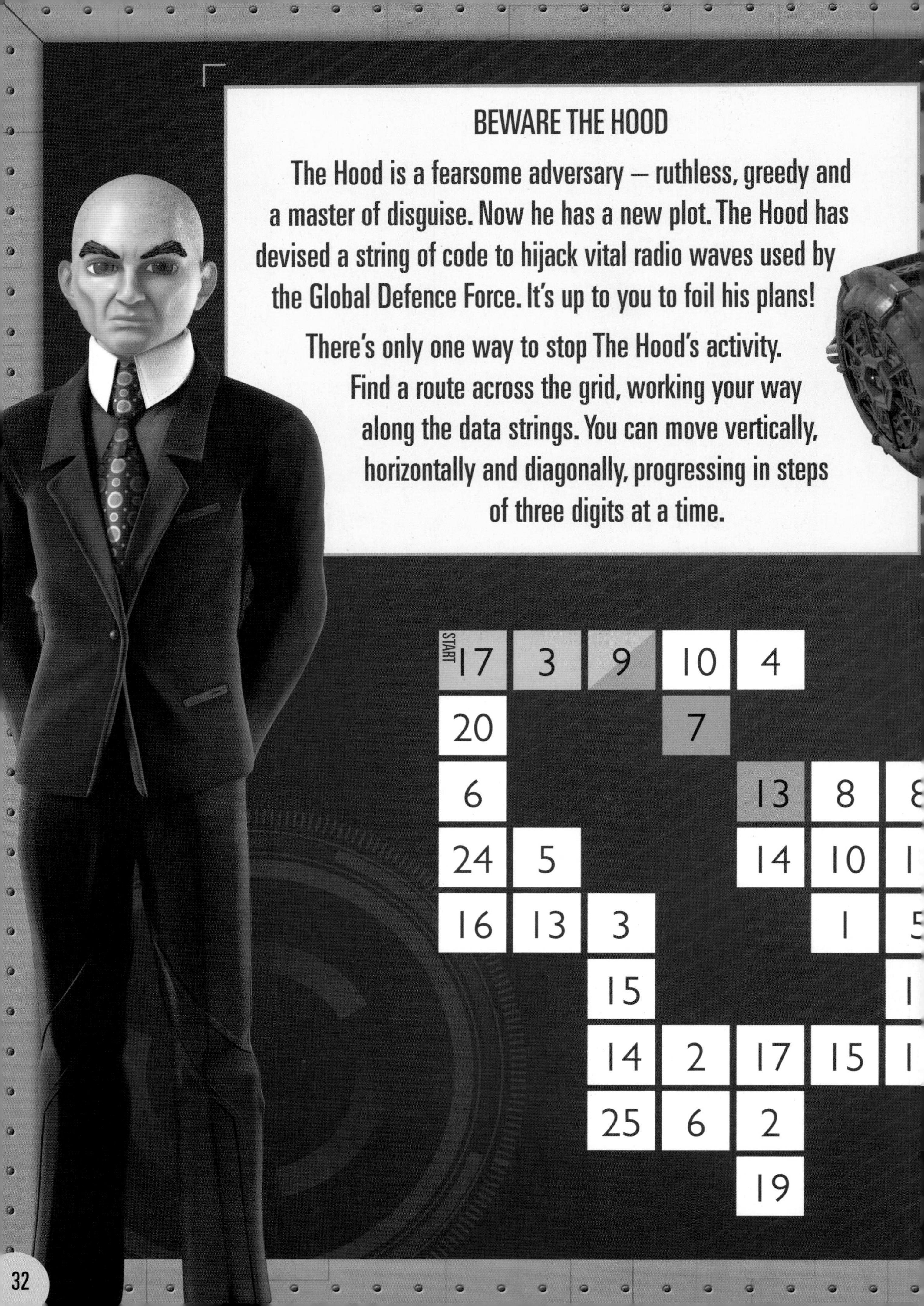

BEWARE THE HOOD

The Hood is a fearsome adversary – ruthless, greedy and a master of disguise. Now he has a new plot. The Hood has devised a string of code to hijack vital radio waves used by the Global Defence Force. It's up to you to foil his plans!

There's only one way to stop The Hood's activity. Find a route across the grid, working your way along the data strings. You can move vertically, horizontally and diagonally, progressing in steps of three digits at a time.

START 17	3	9	10	4	
20			7		
6				13	8
24	5			14	10
16	13	3			1
		15			
		14	2	17	15
		25	6	2	
				19	

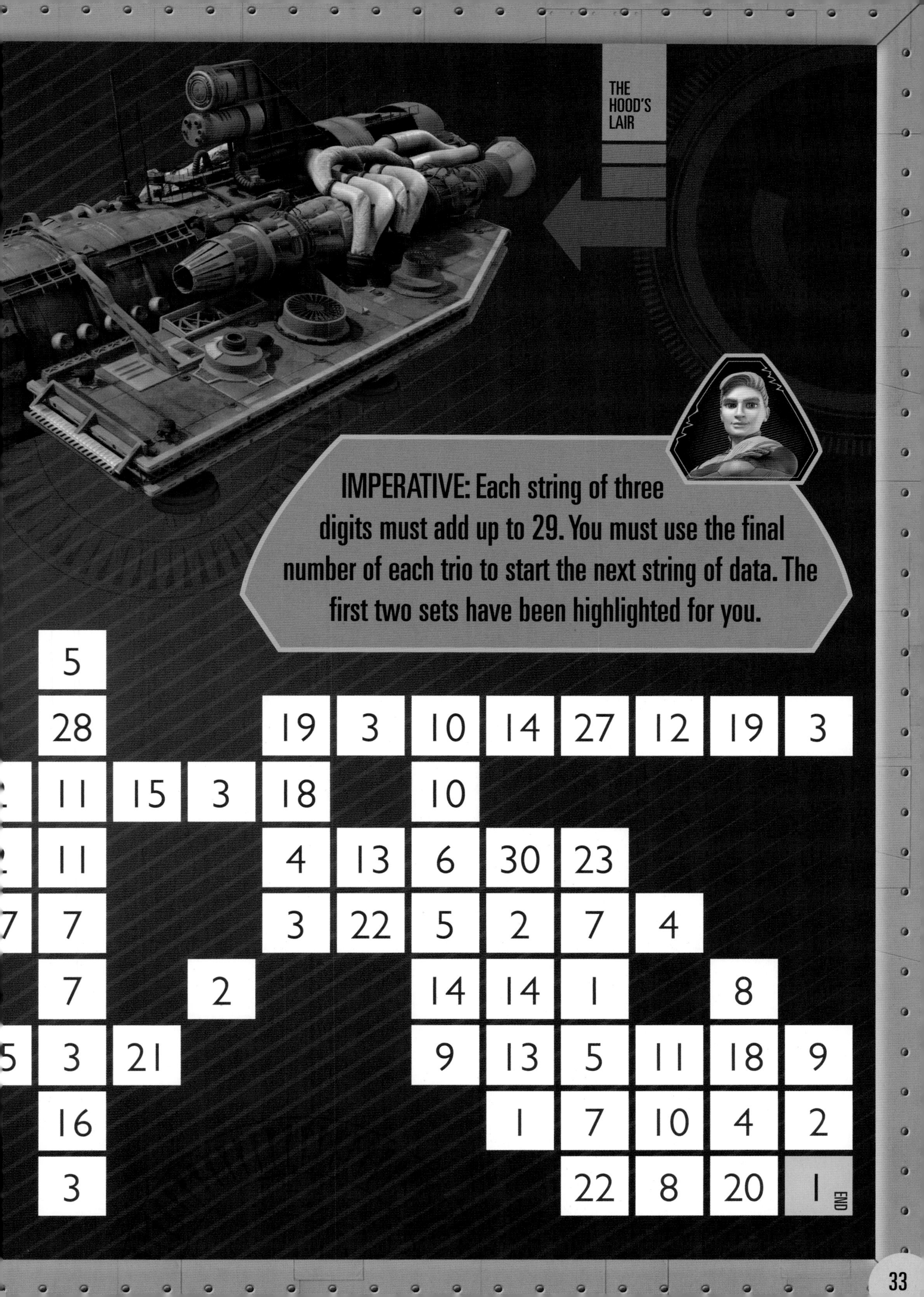
THE HOOD'S LAIR
IMPERATIVE: Each string of three digits must add up to 29. You must use the final number of each trio to start the next string of data. The first two sets have been highlighted for you.
5
28 19 3 10 14 27 12 19 3
11 15 3 18 10
11 4 13 6 30 23
7 7 3 22 5 2 7 4
7 2 14 14 1 8
5 3 21 9 13 5 11 18 9
16 1 7 10 4 2
3 22 8 20 1
END

DROP AND GO

The Tracy brothers don't hesitate, they jump in! Stick a mini poster into the frame, then colour the big picture. Can you match it exactly?

TRUTH OR LIES?

Despite her glamorous status as a London socialite, Lady Penelope always keeps her cool. Many have tried, and failed, to trick the agent into giving away intelligence on International Rescue. How well would you fare under interrogation? Sit down in a quiet place, then read each of these statements. Tick the boxes with a pencil to sort the truth from the lies.

1. Parker's first name is Aloysius.
TRUTH ☐ LIE ☐

2. Colonel Casey would like to see International Rescue disbanded.
TRUTH ☐ LIE ☐

3. International Rescue works for the GDF.
TRUTH ☐ LIE ☐

4. M.A.X. stands for Motorised Autobot eXperimental.
TRUTH ☐ LIE ☐

5. Tracy Island is protected by both holographic and physical cloaking.
TRUTH ☐ LIE ☐

6. Thunderbird 2 is atomic-powered.
TRUTH ☐ LIE ☐

7. Kayo has only been living on Tracy Island for six months.
TRUTH ☐ LIE ☐

8. Thunderbird 5 is connected to Tracy Island via a space elevator.
TRUTH ☐ LIE ☐

9. Gordon is the most gifted pilot on the Thunderbird team.
TRUTH ☐ LIE ☐

10. Thunderbird 5 is constructed around a rotating gravity ring.
TRUTH ☐ LIE ☐

DOWN TIME

Even IR needs a little R&R every now and then! The team likes to chillax in the Tracy Villa – a sleek modern building appointed with cutting edge technology. Use your stickers to show the Tracy brothers enjoying some rare time off-duty.

UNDER PRESSURE

The world is a big place when you patrol the skies, land and sea! Read this account of a breathtaking ocean adventure, then stick in the missing pictures.

1. Thunderbird 5 was orbiting the planet when an SOS signal came through – a fire had been reported in a Heavy Metal Extraction Platform operating on the seabed! John raised the alarm. This was a job for Virgil and Gordon.

4. A little while later, Gordon and Virgil were getting close to the extraction platform. Gordon jumped into Thunderbird 4, then made contact with Ned, the one-man crew trapped on the rig. The fire was spreading fast!

5. Thunderbird 4's robotic claw carefully released an airlock on the side of the platform. Water rushed in, putting out the fire. But before Gordon could save Ned, the platform began to tumble towards an undersea abyss!

8. Down on the platform, things were getting desperate. Virgil shot Thunderbird 2's magnetic grappling cable down into the water. Working with Thunderbird 4, he hooked the crewman's compartment and lifted it to safety.

9. The Hood's henchmen were going all-out to put the brakes on FAB 1. Parker flicked a switch. Suddenly their pursuer found himself thrown to the ground, alone and helpless. Lady Penelope smiled. She had a few questions to ask.

2. While his brothers sprang into action, John informed Hector Ambro, the owner of the platform. Ambro seemed more interested in the toxic waste on-board than the safety of the crewman manning the rig.

3. Something didn't feel right. John put a video-call into FAB 1. He asked Lady Penelope to take a look into Ambro's business, Hydrexler. International Rescue needed to find out what Ambro had planned for all that toxic waste.

6. Above ground, John and Lady Penelope's inquiries took a turn for the worse. Hector Ambro and his business seemed to be merely a cover for something much more sinister. Did The Hood have a hand in Hydrexler's activities?

7. Lady Penelope was right. Before she could delve further, The Hood dispatched a fleet of masked operatives to take out FAB 1! The motorcyclists tried to slash the tyres on the pink limousine.

10. Later the team regrouped at Tracy Island. Gordon and Virgil reported how they had saved the platform's toxic waste from falling into the abyss. Lady Penelope smiled. The Hood's latest plot had been well and truly foiled!

DARK SECRET

Kayo's grudge against The Hood runs deep. The pair share a connection – a secret bond that only Grandma Tracy knows about. Can you work out what place The Hood holds in Kayo's history? Use the clues to fill in the letter grid. When you have finished, read down the blue squares, then write the answer underneath.

1. Parker's primary role for International Rescue.

2. A large space housing the Thunderbird crafts.

3. The southern ocean where Tracy Island is located.

4. Thunderbird 2's pilot.

5. The colour of Thunderbird 1's body.

1									
			2						
			3						
4									
			5						

The Hood is Kayo's _ _ _ _ _

MISSION: CLASSIFIED

Colonel Casey needs to enlist the urgent help of an International Rescue operative. The mission is so secret she cannot use the usual comms devices to brief them. Can you help the GDF make contact with the correct agent? Look at the clues, then use your powers of logic and elimination to select the right person.

1. The operative is related to Jeff Tracy.
2. The operative has fair hair.
3. The operative is the youngest member of International Rescue.

The required operative is:

Stick their picture here.

CROSSCUT

Scott is on a race to stay alive! He is trapped in an old, but highly unstable, uranium mine. He is tasked with locating the only survivor in the mine and then leading them to safety. There isn't a second to lose.

Place the tip of your pencil next to Scott, then trace a route through the gloomy underground corridors. How quickly can you make it to the exit?

IMPERATIVE: You cannot exit the mine until you have passed through the chamber where Marion Van Arkel is trapped!

START

FINISH

ALL-SEEING EYE

Even though he spends his days 54,000 km up in the sky, John keeps a close eye on activity on Earth.

From the observation deck on Thunderbird 5, he can view real time visuals at any time of day or night.

Take a look at the extreme zoomed-in views on John's 360° monitor screens. Can you work out what is being shown in each frame? Draw a line to match each screen to the correct description.

1

2

5

6

A
Kayo test flies a new supersonic airliner.
B
Scott negotiates a zipline.
C
Grandma Tracy has been baking again!
D
Thunderbird 3 goes on space junk clearing duty.
E
Thunderbird 2 deploys the mole POD.
F
M.A.X. is deployed.
G
FAB 1 is airborne.
H
Gordon and Virgil discuss rescue strategies.
3
4
7
8

BRAINS' BLUEPRINT

Brains is inspired by possibilities and the future – if he can dream it, he can build it! Do you have any inventions up your sleeve? The engineer would love to see your work! Use this space to draw sketches and diagrams of your prototype. Don't forget to add labels and give it a name, too.

ANSWERS

Pages 2-3: WE HAVE A SITUATION

5 – GLOBAL DEFENCE FORCE

4 – The two youths must get in the raft and paddle to the mainland. When they reach the shore one must jump out, whilst the other rows back to the island and gets out. The man must now get into the raft and ride back to the mainland. When he is safe, it is his turn to get out so that the youth can climb back on the raft again and paddle back to the island. Now the two lighter individuals are free to travel safely to the mainland together. Mission accomplished.

2 – 1. C, 2. A, 3. D, 4. B

1 – 1. B, 2. B, 3. D

Page 4: THUNDERBIRDS ARE GO!

1. Alan Tracy

2. Scott Tracy

3. Gordon Tracy

Page 5: SECURITY BREACH

It's The Hood!
Pieces: 5, 7, 8, 9

Page 6: TUNNELS OF TIME

The rescue location is: G

Pages 7-8: RING OF FIRE

1. 3	2. Blue
3. A plate	4. John
5. Gordon	6. 6
7. Orange	8. Boots

Page 9: F.A.B.

1. LADY PENELOPE
2. SHERBERT
3.PARKER
4. FAB 1

Pages 10-11: SPACE SPECS

THUNDERBIRD 3
3, 5, 7, 9, 12, 14.

THUNDERBIRD 5
1, 2, 4, 6, 8, 10, 11, 13.

Page 12: GADGET GRID

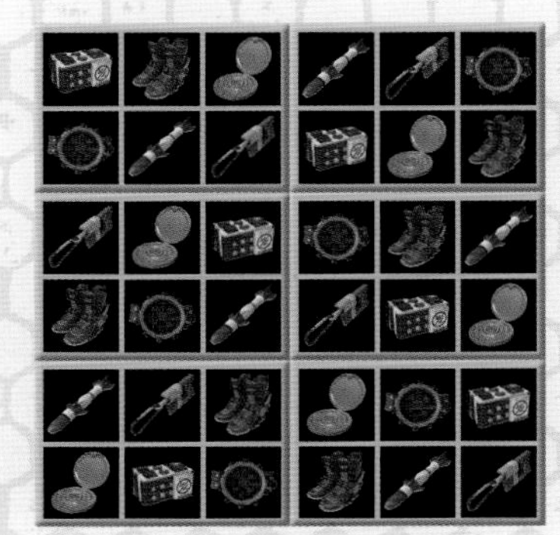

3: DOUBLECROSSER

Message: WAIT FOR HELP

Page 16: COVERT OPS

1. A	2. D	3. C	4. C
5. A	6. D	7. C	8. B

Page 17: AERIAL ASSISTANCE

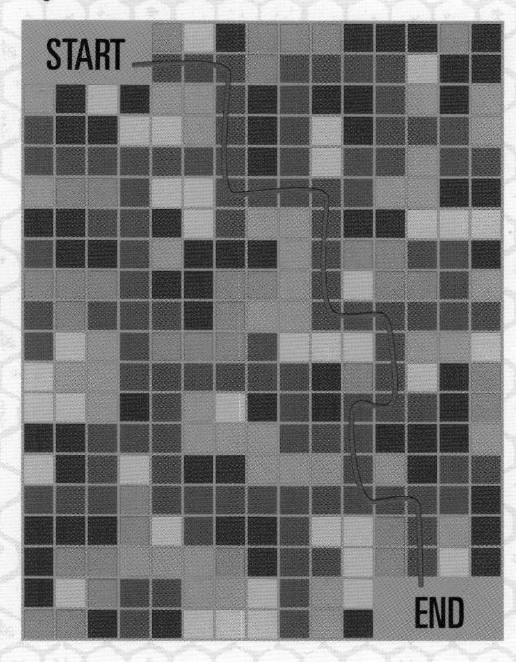

Pages 18-19: PRIVATE AND CONFIDENTIAL

1. VIRGIL	2. COLONEL CASEY	3. TEAPOT
4. GRANDMA	5. BRIEFCASE	6. BOOTS
7. ALAN	8. ROCKET	9. PARKER
10. LUGGAGE	11. MAX	12. SCOTT
13. FAB1	14. SNOW POD	15. GORDON
16. THE HOOD	17. BRAINS	18. JOHN
19. LADY PENELOPE	20. FLOWER	21. COMPACT
22. BROOCH	23. SATCHEL	24. KAYO

INTERNATIONAL RESCUE WAS FOUNDED BY JEFF TRACY.

Pages 20-21: SKY HOOK

1

4

6

Pages 22: SYSTEM CRASH

1. Parker
2. Grandma Tracy
3. Brains
4. Alan Tracy
5. The Hood
6. Kayo

Pages 24-25: KEEP YOUR COOL

Across:		Down:	
	1. Missing		1. Cooking
	2. Virgil		2. Colonel Casey
	3. Rescue		3. Engineer
	4. Compact		4. Five
	5. Volcano		5. Space
	6. Sherbert		6. Scott
	7. Soldier		7. Naps
	8. Kayo		8. Global
	9. Sea		9. British
	10. Pink		10. EOS

Page 26: SECRET SURVEILLANCE

1. "International Rescue, we have a situation!" – JOHN
2. "Yes, M'lady." – PARKER
3. "Time for some heavy lifting!" – VIRGIL
4. "When there's time to lean, there's time to clean!" – GRANDMA TRACY
5. "International Rescue, soon you will be in my hands." – THE HOOD
6. "Nothing's impossible with science!" – BRAINS
7. "This is rather distressing." – LADY PENELOPE
8. "Spoiling your plans is the best part of my job." – KAYO

Page 27: SPACE RACE

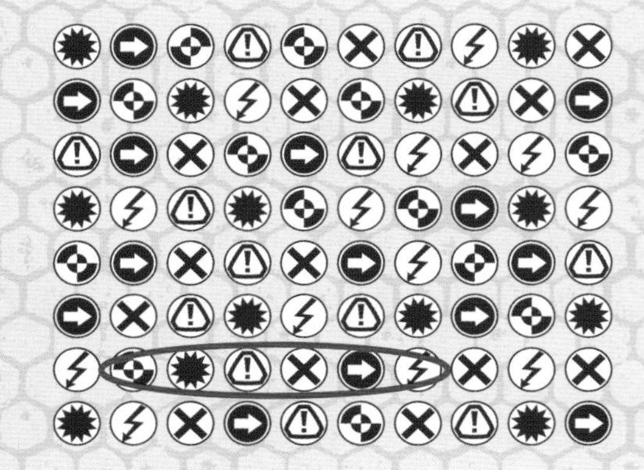

PAGES 28-29: SCRAMBLE!

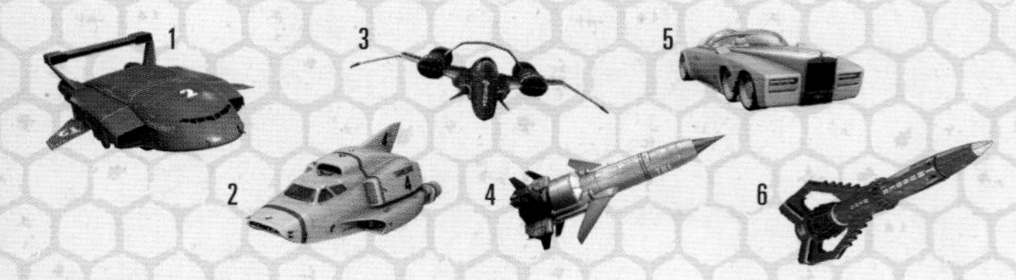

Page 30: BRAIN BURN

PLAN → PLAY → PLOY → PLOT → SLOT → SLAT → SEAT

Page 31: STICKER THIS!

Pages 32-33: BEWARE THE HOOD

17	3	9	10	4				5										
20			7					28			19	3	10	14	27	12	19	3
6				13	8	8	2	11	15	3	18		10					
24	5			14	10	16	2	11			4	13	6	30	23			
16	13	3			1	5	17	7			3	22	5	2	7	4		
		15				12		7		2			14	14	1		8	
		14	2	17	15	18	15	3	21				9	13	5	11	18	9
		25	6	2				16						1	7	10	4	2
				19				3							22	8	20	1

Page 35: TRUTH OR LIES?

1. TRUTH
2. LIE – Colonel Casey is a friend and supporter of International Rescue.
3. LIE – International Rescue's prime function is to rescue when all other methods have failed.
4. LIE – M.A.X. stands for Mechanical Assistant eXperimental
5. TRUTH
6. TRUTH
7. LIE – Kayo grew up on Tracy Island.
8. TRUTH
9. LIE – It's Alan.
10. TRUTH

Pages 38-39: UNDER PRESSURE

6

8

10

Page 40: DARK SECRET

The Hood is Kayo's UNCLE.

Page 41: MISSION: CLASSIFIED

Alan Tracy is the correct operative.

Pages 42-43: CROSSCUT

Pages 44-45: ALL-SEEING EYE

1 = H 2 = E 3 = B 4 = F

5 = G 6 = A 7 = D 8 = C